I Hear the Day

I Hear the Day

Written by
Catherine D. Johnston

Illustrated by Joe Mark

The Merriam-Eddy Company

Published by The Merriam-Eddy Company
South Waterford, Maine
Copyright © 1977 by The Merriam-Eddy Company

Hardcover Edition
ISBN: 0-914562-04-5

Workbook Edition
ISBN: 0-914562-05-3

'79 11388

BFF

Hi!

My name is Wes.

I'm special in a special way.

I wear a hearing aid.

My daddy wears glasses.

My friend Tom wears special shoes.

But I, . . .
I wear a hearing aid.

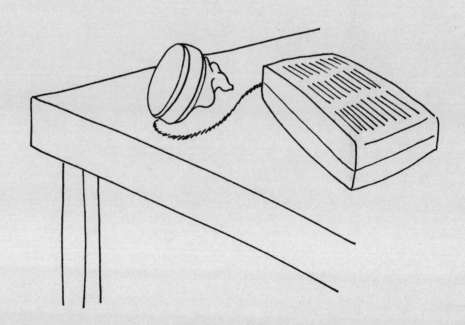

When I get up
in the morning,
I put on my shirt,

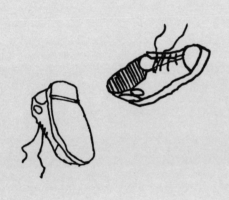

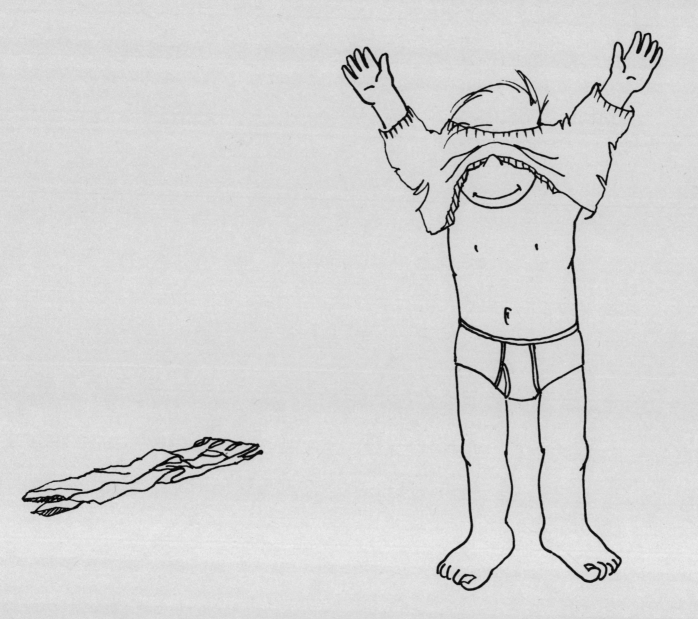

5

and my pants,

and my socks and shoes,

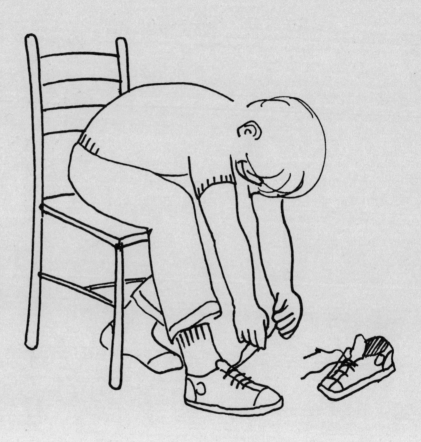

and my hearing aid.

When I put on
the hearing aid,
I test it,
just to see
if it sounds right.

Sometimes I take my aid apart.
It has an ear mold
just made to the size
of my ear,

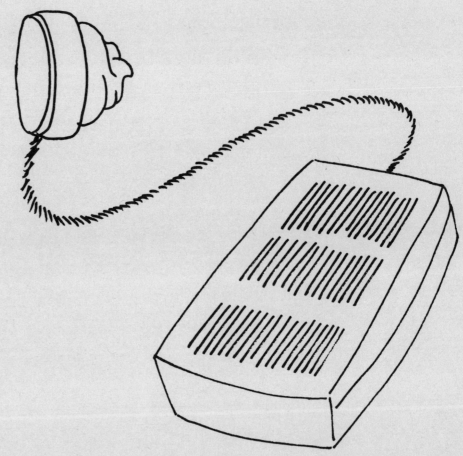

and a receiver
that catches sounds
my ear doesn't,
and a cord.

My aid also has a little box
with a microphone in it
to make sounds louder.
I carry it in a pocket
on the front of me.

Sometimes I chew the cord
when it gets in my way.

Mommy doesn't like that very much.

When I put on my hearing aid,
I hear all my friends.
I listen to a cow say
mooo, mooo.

I listen to a pig say
oink, oink.

I listen to a bird say
tweet, tweet, tweet.

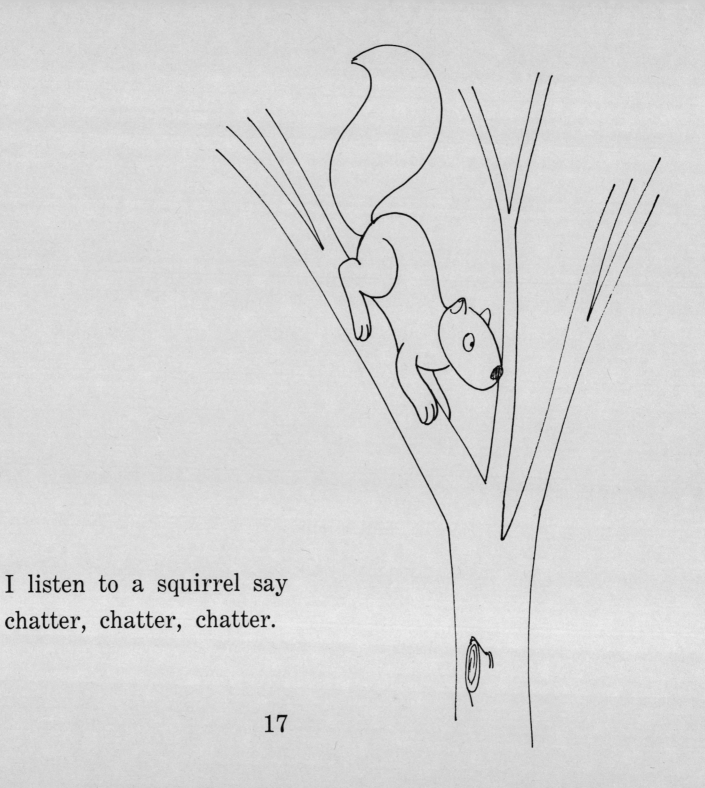

I listen to a squirrel say
chatter, chatter, chatter.

17

And I listen to my mommy say
Wes, Wes, WES!
Sometimes I let her
say it three times
just for fun.

19

With my hearing aid on,
I talk to my friends.
I say moo, moo
to the cow.

I say oink, oink, oink
to the pig.

I say tweet, tweet, tweet
to the bird.

I say chatter, chatter,
chatter to the squirrel.

23

I say Mama to my mommy,
and Dada to my daddy,
and lots of other things.

I listen to the cars
brrr, brrr, brrr
down the street,

and the motorcycle's loud
brooom, brooom.

And the telephone,
ring, ring, ring.

And the knock at the door,
knock, knock, knock.

When night comes,
I take off my shirt,
and my pants,

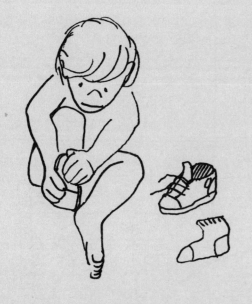

and my shoes and socks,
and my hearing aid.

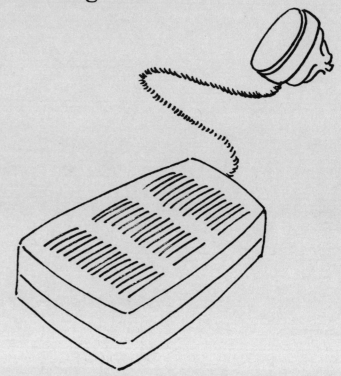

Everything is quiet.
Shhhh.

Everything is different now
and kind of scary.
Shhh, shhh, shhhh.

I remember my friends,
and I go to sleep.

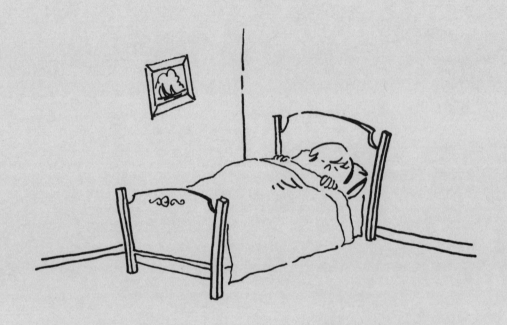

Good night!